LADY FAÇADE

OUT OF THE ASHES

A STORY OF SURVIVAL

LADY FAÇADE

OUT OF THE ASHES

A STORY OF SURVIVAL

SBPC

SIMMS BOOKS PUBLISHING CORPORATION

SBPC

SIMMS BOOKS PUBLISHING CORP.

Publishers Since 2012

Published by Simms Books Publishing Corporation

Jonesboro, GA

Library of Congress Cataloging in Publication Data

2020916830

OUT OF THE ASHES

LADY FAÇADE

ISBN: 978-1-949433-09-8

Printed in the United States of America

Book Arrangement by Simms Books Publishing

Mary Hoekstra Editor

DEDICATION

I dedicate this book first to my Father which is in heaven, and to all the girls, young ladies, women, boys, young men, and men going through or having been through abuse, whether it was sexual, physical, mental, verbal, emotional, or many kinds.

To my earthly father, whom I'm hoping is in heaven, please forgive me for hating you so much, first for abusing my mother and your wrongdoings, and second, for not being there for me when I needed you most.

To my grandmother, I love you for being a strong tower.

Also, to my brother, whom I know is in heaven, thank you for introducing me to the Holy Spirit. Without it, this book wouldn't be possible. See you when I walk through the Pearly Gates.

FOREWORD

11) For I know the plans I have for you, declares the
LORD, plans to prosper you and not to harm you,
to give you a future and a hope 12) Then you will call upon
Me and come and pray to Me, and I will listen to you
Jeremiah: 29:11-12

I am a firm believer that God has already pre-determined our destiny and endpoints in life. This concept sounds great, powerful, but it is sometimes hard to wrap our minds around. What really makes believing our destiny is set, is all the difficult and challenging things we go through in this life.

How can God have something good at the end for me, when I face Hell, misery, pain, and abuse? This question is especially difficult when you are young.

In my life, I have come to learn that despite all the difficult things we face, God still has a plan for us. Nothing we face in life has the power to erase or alter the good, acceptable, and perfect will of God for our lives.

God knows this principle but so does the enemy of our souls! Satan knows he cannot stop you himself from reaching your endpoint in life, however, he works to make sure that things happen in our lives that threaten and sometimes succeed in making us prisoners to bondage, addiction, toxic relationships, and harmful behaviors.

Never forget: The issue in life is not about whether you will make it to your destiny, but rather the time, speed, path, and condition you will arrive at your divine endpoint. The enemy targets and goes after gifted young people to try to give them baggage attached to their purpose that drags them down, weighs them down, slows them down, and can even stop them from taking another God-directed step.

When I was a young child, I had a strong sense of what I thought my purpose in life was supposed to be. This was an amazing occurrence, because of all the obstacles and challenges I had to face at an early age. Really, before I was even born into the world, there was a plot to stop my entrance. Since that point, it seemed that attack after attack, ranging from being diagnosed as mentally retarded at the age of 3, to fighting learning disabilities and overcoming severe stuttering and delayed speech, became my portion.

How could a little Black boy who could barely put a sentence together be anything significant in life? Thankfully, I got a glimpse of my purpose early.

This sense of purpose was so powerful that the painful, disappointing, and seemingly hindering experiences in my life were never strong enough to kill my destiny! This became even so much more vital to my life's journey when I came to the tough reality that my issues and struggles from things, I endured in my childhood could never stop God's love for me or His purpose for my life.

However, I had to learn to forgive, I had to be healed, and I had to learn to manage the scars I bore, so I would not be living on purpose yet be bound to chains of my past.

I ask you a serious question as you read this book: Do you know your God-given purpose? The reality is, that PURPOSE is powerful, but only if you know what it is and you believe and live it the same as what God intends. Also, purpose is only effective if you make the decision to take off the masks and get real with yourself about what you are dealing with.

One of best gifts you can give yourself is self-awareness. Many people ignore what is happening on the inside of them. They go on blindly, trying to walk through this life, in hopes they will make it to that place God designed for them. Others want to be free, healed, and delivered, but have no idea where to start!

But there is hope! If you are not aware and are unsure about how to live a life on purpose, fueled by forgiveness, healing, and self-acceptance, this book is for you.

The author of this book, Lady Façade, is the epitome of a woman who has been through some of the toughest situations in her life yet has taken control of her life with the help of the Holy Spirit. She is now making a great impact for the Kingdom of God in the lives of many women. During the time I have had the pleasure of being her overseer, I have personally witnessed her fight to gain greater self-awareness, courage, and determination to be healed, to walk in forgiveness, and to make decisions that would push her towards God's purpose.

One of the things I respect most deeply about Lady Façade is that she is not ashamed of her story or of her journey. She recognizes that all the pain and abuse she endured were necessary in forming her into the woman of God she is today.

The same applies to you! I pray that the chains of shame, guilt, and self-hatred will break off your life in a powerful way. I am absolutely confident of this fact about you: You are way too valuable and important to God and the world to be unaware of your purpose, and to not be delivered from all the things in your past that have wounded you.

As you read this book, may you remain open to what God has to say, and experience the healing power that comes from removing the façade and being a free, healed, and delivered person!

In Christ's Power,

Apostle Dr. David E. Jackson

President/Overseer

The Rock, ATL

Atlanta, GA

www.dejackson.org

EDITOR'S FOREWORD

When she speaks, her words are wise, and she gives
instructions with kindness. Proverbs 31:26

I make my living with words, the words of writers, poets, lyricists, screenwriters, and my own words of fiction, poetry and nonfiction. In all the years I've worked with words, this is only the second time I've asked to write a foreword!

Why do that? Just like you, I don't always believe everything I read. In fact, it takes a lot to convince me to just read, much less believe! There's no reward, because it's not about reward; it's about faith and recommendation.

This small book, from the heart, soul, mind and hands of a remarkable author, was put down on these pages because of God's command to her. As you'll soon learn, there were times in Lady Façade's life when God's command to take another breath, take another step, take another look, take another direction, were what kept her alive and moving forward. And what kept her moving forward was God's love.

Yes, Lady Façade is a survivor; that means she didn't die and, believe me, that is a miracle, as you'll soon read. Survivors who see the extraordinary blessing they've been given to survive realize, as has Lady Façade, that there is another level they have to climb.

This book is about victory. It is Lady Façade's story for your victory and to glorify God. As her words worked in me, and as I worked on them and got to know her, I came to respect and love her courage, single-mindedness, and faith…and, of course, her words! It has been an honor to work with her and her words.

I pray you will open your mind, heart and soul and let her words work in you so you achieve God's message for your life and achieve God's victory for your life. That is how we live His life within us.

Mary Hoekstra, Editor

26 August 2020

INTRODUCTION

I wrote this book to get to the root of the problems of unforgiving hearts. I wrote it to let you know that harboring hurt and pain is like holding onto a cancer eating away at you; it's like keeping hold of a self-inflicted wound. You are punishing yourself by harming your own body, heart, mind and soul.

When you feel that you are the only one going through pain, abuse, injury, and torment, remember there is always someone who is going through all those trials in ways that are worse than your situation. But there is new light, new hope, a way to step into a new life.

Jesus Christ can heal all your wounds if you trust in Him and allow Him to plant the seed of love in your heart. The seed of love will uproot the manifestation of bitterness and resentment.

Don't hold back, it's not your fault you were, or are, being abused, even if you are told that it is. Even if you are warned not to tell, for whatever reason the predator comes up with, even if he/she says they will kill your mom or anyone else you love, this is only the predator's excuse for not to get caught themselves.

You are a victim and you could stop a cycle of rape, molestation, or incest. The fact of the matter is, God made you and allowed things to happen to you and in your life for this reason: To help someone else overcome. Most important, He allowed things to happen to you so God will get the glory!

WHAT LOVE IS

L-O-V-E: Love endures long and is patient and kind,

love never is envious nor boils over with jealousy,

love is not boastful or vainglorious, does not display itself haughtily.

Love is not conceited – arrogant and inflated with pride,

love is not rude (unmannerly) and does not act unbecomingly.

God's love in us does not insist on its own rights or its own way, for it is not self-seeking, it is not touchy or fretful or resentful,

love takes no account of the evil done to it—pays no attention to a suffered wrong.

Love does not rejoice at injustice and unrighteousness but rejoices when right and truth prevail.

Love bears up under anything and everything that comes,

love is ready to believe the best of every person,

love's hopes are fadeless under all circumstances and it endures everything [without weakening].

Love never fails– never fades out or becomes obsolete or comes to an end.

Based upon 1Corinthians 13:4-8 (The Amplified Bible)

You are a love creature. Only allow people to love and support you from their hearts. I pray you will always have the common sense, as a creature of love, to know the difference between people who really love you from their hearts, compared to those who only use the word, "love," as a weapon or worse yet, use the word "love" as an empty expression.

12)Put on therefore, as God's elect, holy and beloved, a heart of compassion, kindness, lowliness, meekness, longsuffering; 13) forbearing one another, and forgiving one another, if any many have a complaint against any; even as the Lord forgave you, so also do ye; 14) and above all these things put on love, which is the bond of perfectness. 15) And let the peace of Christ rule in your hearts, to which also ye were called in one body; and be ye thankful. Colossians 3:12-1

Chapter 1

This little ole house

They say home is where the heart is, where you should feel safe. They say home is those four walls of security, shelter, and a place to lay your head. My family shared this little house together, my mother, father, my five siblings, and we even had extended family members who stayed downstairs from us in the same apartment building. We were surrounded by family.

Imagine growing up in a world where you had no worries. All you wanted and desired was given to you. As a child, you had experiences that you will remember for the rest of your life and they are all filled with love and joy. You were loved protected and inspired to do well in life, because your parents and community had built a safety net around you so you would succeed and flourish.

You never had to worry about anyone doing something bad, taking your innocence, abusing you, and taking your precious youth from you.

I can only imagine what that must have been like...

I was born in a small town in the upper Midwest. My earliest memories of childhood and the place that I called

1

home were chaotic, traumatizing, impressionable, and they would span a lifetime of pain.

I can remember, to this day, how my house was set up, the décor, everything, just as though I was standing in it at this moment. I can clearly see the small apartment we stayed in. Up the stairs to the left was the living room with a small, old-fashioned stove. To the right was my parents' room and going back further to the front of the apartment was the bathroom. To the left and next to it was our room. The memories that came out of that house...oh boy, if the walls could talk.

I remembered the kitchen...wow, the smells the sights and sounds. My mother would make the best food out of that little kitchen. She also had a great sense of style. She kept the house clean, organized and decked out. I remember this red chain lamp with a marble bottom; it almost reminded me of a royal crown.

The bunkbeds in our room bring back memories also, and not good ones. I likened those bunkbeds not as a place of comfort, but a place of molestation and abuse. They were no refuge, no place to sleep and dream at the end of the day. Remembering the little things, the details of them, have all played out in my mind, over and over again. I could not escape them, yet I tried.

I remember, from a very young age, the house I had grown to love would be the house I would grow to hate. It became the house of the violence that would dominate my little soul.

It all started, from my first memory of that violence, with my mother being beat by my father. Sitting in that house I could hear a loud commotion outside. We rushed to look out the window, then to the door, to see what was going on. It was my mother and father arguing. They came into the house and I followed them to the bathroom. Sitting on the toilet, I got a bird's-eye view of what pain and violence looked like and the end results.

I remember seeing my mother leaning over the sink, with blood pouring out of her face. My father stood by her. In the deafening screams and cries from my mother, I could feel both of their energies. He was filled with anger and she was both angry and full of fear. I could feel it at that moment and that type of fear paralyzes you; you can do nothing but be still.

That would not be the end of those types of moments, because we all would experience such moments just about every week, growing up in that little apartment.

Just like all other children, we tried to make the most of a bad situation and we did what children do...we played. I remember, one time, one of my dad's friends caught us outside playing. He told on us to our father and we were punished severely, but he, the friend of my father, was rewarded with a beer for telling on us.

We played like most children do, but once one of my brothers was chasing a mouse with my cousins and he fell. A nail went into his forehead and my dad and uncle used a hammer to take it out. To this day, my brother bears a scar in his forehead from that incident. Funny thing, though, his daughter has a scar in her forehead that looks similar. I guess kids will be kids.

A double minded man is unstable in all his ways.

James 1:8

Chapter 2

Being my father's child

I know only a few things about my father because he died at the early age of 28 from emphysema, but the things I do remember I can never forget. My father was both physically and mentally abusive to us and to our mother. I've always wondered, looking back, how he could do this to her. She gave him six children. Why would he beat her?

I loved my father, as a young girl should, but it became a complicated situation, to say the least. My father would take risks when he was driving down a road coming back to the house from out of town. He would drive without the lights on from time to time, which drove my mother crazy. She would yell at him, pleading that he turn the lights on before he crashed.

I learned that my father had been in prison for two years after shooting the grandfather of one of my close friends. One day, we had come back from the laundry mat, and while taking the clothes upstairs and heading to the bathroom I heard a loud bang. Apparently, my friend's grandfather, or someone, was out for blood and revenge and shot at our parent's bedroom window.

I was so shaken up that I peed on myself and had nightmares from that day forward. My mother would ask who peed the bed and sometimes my siblings would be blamed, but it was me. I would pee in the bed because I was scared to go to the bathroom, fearing that the loud shot would happen again.

As a child, I had no answers, we were all victims of those who were supposed to watch us and love us.

My father had some demons in him that he was fighting and it showed. I always wondered why. I remember how he would speak to my mother and to us, when and if we got out of line. I didn't have a long time with him, being that he died at such a young age. Looking back, I would say that he had a hard life that ultimately took him at an early age.

I don't remember if he was on drugs or not, but I do remember how he would get when he had too much to drink. It seems, at times, he would be oblivious to what was going on with his children.

I remember, when we had babysitters, they would touch us and threaten us to not tell anyone. As a child, what do you do when you are threatened and someone says that they will kill your parents if you tell on them?

My own father would beat me when I refused to sit on my grandfather's lap. He thought I was being disrespectful, but there was something else going on. I remember my grandfather would grind on me when I was sitting on his lap. He even fondled me and a close family member on a picnic table behind the house.

I recall the abuse vividly from when I was a little older. I was in a room alone with my grandfather and he was fondling me and on top of me, and I remember the door opened and it was my grandmother. She didn't stop him at all, just told him, "Don't hurt her." She closed the door, and he continued. I know now that she must have been scared of him, and he only did what he was taught out of slavery.

I remember my family going back and forth from one town to another in the state where I was born. We would travel the back roads. During those trips, my father would drive part of the road with the lights off, which, as I said, scared my mother. I found it rather amusing as a child and when I got old enough to drive, I tried this same stunt once or twice on the same street! We pick up things naturally as a force of habit; monkey see monkey do.

When my father began to get real sick, a lot of changes started happening in our house. We could feel the shift in the house, and we started to get in trouble for no reason at all. We (the children) had started to build resentment toward our father from all the things that we saw, heard, and went through.

There was a big, green oxygen tank in the house and the tubes were in my father's nose. We could hear him sucking air from time to time when he had his bad days.

One time, me and my brother had gotten in trouble again. I remember my father hitting me and we wished that he would die. I lied to my daddy about writing a curse word on the wall that started with an "s" and ended with a "t." He asked me and one of my brothers who did it and we both said no, it wasn't us. I guess it was the way I said it that made him slap me. I think shortly after that moment Daddy went downstairs and I was crying. My brother and I looked at each other and said, "I hope he dies." You have to be careful how you speak; it can become witchcraft.

A couple weeks later, my dad was in the hospital. Someone was asking my aunt about my dad, and this female who is related on my dad's side, said he was going to "d-i-e" (spelling it), and I said, "He's not going to die." Sure enough, shortly after that, or it could have been weeks, my mom was upstairs and got a phone call, I could see her in agony with one boot unzipped. She was trying to pull herself together as she waited on the sitter to come watch us so she could go to the hospital.

The morning of my father's funeral I remember listening to my mother. She cried, both loud and with a small whimper. Me and my other siblings were getting ourselves together. We all had new clothes and our hair was done the night before.

I remember, like it was yesterday, how we all came together. Here we were at the funeral home. While the obituary was being read, when I heard my name, I smiled for whatever reason. My mom was not doing well, so one of my uncles picked her up and carried her outside to the car.

During his service, I reminisced about my father, the good, the bad, and the ugly, not knowing how losing him would have a damning effect on my life. Yes, he had his issues but he still loved his children and would protect us at all costs. I didn't realize it at that young age. I was confused, not knowing if I was happy he was gone or sad that he was gone.

"I hereby command you: Be strong and courageous; do not be frightened or dismayed, for the LORD your God is with you wherever you go." Joshua 1:9

Chapter 3

Adjusting and weathering the storm

I never thought, later on in life I would miss my dad. In some cases, I wished he could have been around because I needed his protection. My mom had to do what she had to do as a single parent to take care of six children and she was hardly home. Don't get me wrong, I am proud of my mom for her determination and motivation to want to live, press on, and have the best for her children.

All the neighborhood kids used to come to our house. We had everything from tetherball to a pool table. I guess some money had come in from my dad passing away. From what I heard, some family members felt slighted because they had helped my mom up to this point, but when the money came in, they felt like she had forgotten about them. They felt she didn't need their assistance anymore and it put distance between them. They still loved her, they were just not as close as they used to be. I'm sure none of it was intentional, but after she figured it out, it was too late.

The distance affected the children the most. I can remember my uncle and aunt babysitting us, telling us ghost stories and taking good care of us. I love both of them so much and we have always been close.

Let the fun begin! Here we are taking vacations and going to various places like Enchanted Forest, Cedar Point, Kings Island, Sea World and hitting the beaches.

My mom used to throw us big Halloween parties and different events for every occasion. I appreciated it, because it made me a great hostess and event planner to this day. Except for Halloween, now that I know the real meaning. It's a witch festival, October 31, All Hallows Eve....

I remember chanting: "Mary Weather B can't get.... (whoever was in the basement at that time)." Both my siblings and friends used to chant that when they individually locked us in the basement and wouldn't let us out for 30-45 minutes. To this day, one of my siblings is still nerve-shocked behind that.

"Rock a bye baby on the treetop (you know the rest)." Why would you want your baby to fall out of a tree?

Saying the same word at the same time as someone else, then to jinx yourself so you can't talk for how many minutes. All of this is witchcraft but I praise God that I am not held accountable for the things I didn't know as a child.

In our basement, we used to hold our breath and pick one another up to bear hug until we passed out, then get slapped in the face until we awakened. Where did this type of stuff come from? Some questions may never be answered.

During the time that we were adjusting to losing our dad, a close family member started abusing me and, in the end, he was the one who took my virginity. I could feel the pain that never went away, the first hurt of having intercourse and a close family member abusing me. It hurt me badly enough, to the point that the pain would haunt me so strongly, like I could actually feel intercourse taking place after that.

At various times, he would just take it, not knowing I was being raped. I wondered why my mom didn't investigate why we would fight like cats and dogs all the time. When I say he would beat me down like a stranger on the streets, that is how he treated me. Denial made me the problem child. I felt like the black sheep.

Our friends and neighborhood kids would come to our house because my mom was working nights. A lot of sexual activity was going on, even when they would involve our younger siblings.

From this point, I felt like a sex magnet, as though familiar and perverse spirits drew themselves to me. I might as well have been wearing a sign that said, "Hey come on and have your way with me, I am available for whatever. Don't worry about my age, take advantage of me."

The curses that follow us haunt our generation: incest, deception, hatred, jezebel, schizophrenia, denial, fault-finding, rage, betrayal, and illiteracy.

When I speak on illiteracy it is to a certain extent. In my immediate family, there are only a few who graduated with a diploma or have gone to college, extending from the limited education my grandparents had. My surviving grandfather can only sign an X for his name to this day.

I started listening to a family member as she was telling me closets kept skeletons, those "what goes on in this house stays in this house" secrets. When I asked my mom or grandma about it, they would say, "No she is lying, she is sick and needs to take her medicine." How should I accept this? And she used to say to me, "Auntie wouldn't lie to you." I always wondered, *who do I believe? My mom wouldn't lie to me, my grandma wouldn't lie to me, right?* I've experienced all of those things my aunt spoke to me about.

They have corrupted themselves, their spot is not the spot
of his children: they are a perverse and crooked
generation. Deuteronomy 32:5

Chapter 4

Troubled Teen Years

I am from a small town in the Midwest where there is a lot of talent, but it is undiscovered, from basketball to vocalists. From the outside looking in, "thirsty" is fairly prejudiced. A lot of our black brothers and sisters were cheated out of scholarships, except for the ones who had an identity crisis. You know what I'm saying without saying. All the while, deep, dark secrets, sex, molestation, and abuse ran rampant and, as children, we do what we have been taught.

In this same apartment where I grew up, someone was molesting us and teaching us about sex. I am visualizing these bunk beds and a single bed, so vivid... Life would never be, and has never been, the same.

*****

They are finally finished and it's time to sneak out the basement. We made it and we didn't get caught. My cousin was in junior high school at this time and I was in elementary.

How on God's green earth did she and the nice guy's older cousin pull off signing me out of school? This happened weeks after our last adventure. This guy was manipulative, persuasive, and addicted to young girls and sex. He was also very handsome and popular in school; he was definitely a ladies' man. Here we go for the ride. I'm not sure where we ended up that day, but I'm sure if he took a risk at the school it had to be well worth it. Me and the nice guy were getting closer and closer. He had begun riding his bike over to see me. But where did it all go wrong and why?

The tables turned and now there were two guys involved, instead of one. There was this grocery store nearby and in the back was a wooded area where they had taken us. It was obvious that my cousin had been to this location before because she knew exactly where the spot was. On the ground were blankets and a clean area, nothing but soft ground. As we began to make out, pants went down, and in the middle of having sex, the older guy yelled out, "Let's switch," so they did. I don't know how I felt after that but I'm sure it wasn't a good feeling; if it had been a good feeling, I would describe it.

Now that the older guy was coming over to the house just as much as the nice guy, there were three guys, the older guy's brother and all three were related to each other. It was me, my cousin, and two close friends, along with our neighborhood friends that we considered brothers and sisters.

We were having sex parties. There was someone for everyone in every room and the basement, excluding younger siblings. Our neighbor at the time knew something was going on, and especially his wife did, as well. Sometimes it pays to have what you believe to be nosy neighbors who cared about your welfare. They saw how much traffic was going in and out, kids and teens everywhere.

My mom started whooping us according to the neighbors' report…extension cords, switches, broom/mop handles, slaps in the face. She even tried babysitters who weren't any better, because she was always with her boyfriend in the basement, entertaining him at the bar, playing music, and we were upstairs.

I still have a scar on the inside of my right thigh next to my "poodle" birth mark, where Momma hit me with an extension cord. (Wow, it just now dawned on me that's the closest thing to a whip!) It actually took a small plug of flesh out my leg. Maybe that is why she changed her weapons.

Sometimes, when our sitter was entertaining in the basement, my older sibling and his friends came up with tying sheets together and pulling people up through the second story window in the back of the house, where the nosy neighbors couldn't see.

Everywhere that I remember, we engaged in sexual activity. In my grandma's house (mom's mom) in the basement on that street where the neighbors watched what was happening. It was a few young teens who were curious about sex, and apparently practicing on each other, and all lived in the same neighborhood. I don't know when it began, but it was happening. Two of the teens were on top of each other on the couch in the basement.

One of the girls used to make me put my mouth on her and point to where she wanted the act performed. Sometimes it would be right after she got out the bathtub and would have me perform the act while she sat on the toilet with the lid down, while I was on my knees. The smell of her vagina haunted me. She was acting out what later was found out to be what someone in her family was doing to her, molesting and abusing her. This cycle of having sex and entertaining older guys had become part of my normal teenage life.

I was now hanging out with older girl cousins at the YMCA, which had a teen night called Super Saturday. *Disco Duck* was a famous hit at that time. Well, one night was when this older guy was interested in me. He was really a nice guy, very polite and mannerly. As the week went by, I was looking forward to walking to the YMCA so I could see my caring friend and dance to *Disco Duck*!

One night, after we were invited to this nice guy's home, we rode with his older cousin in what we thought to be a fancy car back then. My cousin and I and the two guys got out and went inside. I don't remember anything happening with him, but I heard them in the next room. I think I was scared because my mother used to come home early and we would have to hide people in the closets or basement sometimes. She would catch them, but sometimes she wouldn't. I knew the consequences of my actions.

"My people are destroyed for lack of knowledge: because thou hast rejected knowledge, I will also reject thee, that thou shalt be no priest to me: seeing thou hast forgotten the law of thy God, I will also forget thy children." Hosea 4:6

Chapter 5

Young, wild and pregnant

There was someone's aunt who would make us put our mouths on her and we were constantly abused by strangers, my aunt's boyfriend, and others. At 13 years old, I became pregnant and my mom didn't even know I was pregnant.

One day I was on my way to school and I passed out, but nobody knew I was passed out on the street. When I woke up, I was in the ER and my mom and grandmother were around me. I could see a big stomach. I used to dress with a big t-shirt to cover up and no one knew until that day.

I had grown women who were constantly trying to fight me over a boy who was in high school and was about to go to college. They would fight me every day, while I was pregnant. I was in junior high school and my brother was in high school. I would run up to him and he would tell me, "You are a [my family name], you can fight, go back and fight!"

After I had my son, I went to the skating rink and borrowed a lot of the guys' class rings, enough to fill up both my hands. I had this ongoing problem with this one woman, and that day was the day it was going to stop. When I caught up with her, I hit her in the face. I beat her so badly that I left a deep scar on her face after the fight. She never picked on me again.

I began to be rebellious. I had lost my childhood. My friends would go to the pool, to the park, and I had to bring my baby along. I was a child trying to raise a child. I began to fight a lot; I fought just about every day. I was addicted to fighting. They would come get me to beat someone up. I fought for my brothers and for anyone. I fought with weapons, knives, guns, and anything. I didn't care. I even earned a rep for knocking out grown men.

There was a guy who was interested in me and we started going out when I was in the 12th grade. My brother lied and said that someone else was coming to the house, so the guy put his hands on me and we broke up.

I was on my way to jail or someone's graveyard and needed to slow down.

My mom sent me away to the West Coast to live with my aunt. My mom raised my son while I was out there for two and a half years. I was supposed to get a job when I got out there. My mother thought that it would be a good change for me, since my aunt who lived out there was and had her stuff together.

Once I got to the West Coast, I quickly learned that was not the case at all. My aunt was in an abusive relationship with a boyfriend. She and I moved out of his place and went to live with another friend of hers who was a drug addict. Talking about jumping out of the frying pan into the fire! They would free base and do drugs in front of me. My uncle told me to snort a needle drop of drugs, trying to deter me from ever doing drugs.

My situation couldn't get any worse, right? Wrong. Between dealing with my aunt's situation, her boyfriend, and trying to make my life better, I was forced to do what I had to do.

I had started doing something I was all too familiar with, giving my body to complete strangers, this time for money. I frequented the racetrack and turned tricks in the stables to help take care of my son. I was sending what I made back home to my mom; she had no idea what I was really doing. I was in the street with a young white girl who knew the streets. She was only 15 years old and we used to run the streets. She was with the Puerto Rican gang, Los Chellos.

We hung with the gang, a white girl and black girl. One time, we ran into this white biker gang and they kept calling the white girl "a nigger lover." They could not stand to see one of their own hanging with a black girl. During my time in the streets I met so many different kinds of people and did whatever the gang wanted me to do.

I met this white guy named S whose mother was a university professor. He was a good friend of mine, johns and he took good care of me, which helped me put my son through private school. We went on various sprees and I participated in crazy things you wouldn't believe.

S was killed in his mother's condo; the street life had caught up with him. He would be the point in all of our sprees, no matter what it was, cheating johns, robbing them, or hitting jewelry stores. His death took me by surprise and it affected me in a bad way. He had become my friend, my partner in crime, and it was traumatic seeing him lying there dead.

I tried to get it out of my head; I still had a son to raise. The heat was on us after S was killed, I knew it was a matter of time before they came after me. Things started to fall apart, from being robbed to a string of bad luck.

Something had to change. I met a doctor and we would hang out and party. I stole his bracelet and pawned it for $250 and I took the Greyhound and went back to the Midwest.

"I hereby command you: Be strong and courageous; do not be frightened or dismayed, for the LORD your God is with you wherever you go." Deuteronomy 31:6

Chapter 6

Struggling to make a change

I had lived a wild life up to that point and was coming home to get my life back together. Months later, I got pregnant again, this time a baby girl. I was sleeping around and did not know who her father was; it was between two different men, and later I found out the truth. I continued to get into more trouble and became a drug addict.

I put all my responsibility on others and kept running from my obligations. I still had the urge to fight but was not ready for relationships. I was ready for just living a wild life. I was staying in a hotel, trying to teach my daughter how to swim. A near death experience; my son recused me and my daughter from drowning, she panicked and held on to my neck as we both went down, gave me the motivation to do more for my children.

I was still partying and doing drugs. I was crossfading, mixing drugs, addicted to snorting cocaine, smoking primos, cigarettes blotters, christmas trees, acid, blue ladies, and all drugs except heroin. I was a mad alcoholic and when I drank, I was ready to fight! I was independent, but still selling weed and selling dope. I was tired of going back and forth to jail. I was on restriction and not supposed to leave the house, but I did. I got into being a scammer with checks and cards. You name it, I did it.

I moved to another city to give my children a better life. I was working in a car manufacturing plant. I met a guy who was hard on the eyes. I took good care of him and he started to do great things for me. He bought me a car. I didn't like him in that way, but I learned to like him. He started using drugs. I was still selling drugs. He tried to convince me that my children were stealing from me, but that was how I found out that he was doing drugs all along.

He was stealing drugs from me and abusing me. He even pushed me down the stairs. We had a fight one night, and he kept denying he was stealing from me. I got slick with him and we started fighting. I don't remember the whole fight, but when I came to, the landlord found me and called the ambulance.

At the ER, when I woke up, my mom was on my right side, he was on my left side, and my grandmother was there rubbing my feet. I was so weak but I was trying to spit on him. My mom didn't know that he was abusing me during that time.

Those were some trying times in my life. I had to think about my mortality at that time, after being beat so badly from my man, I was hanging on to life and almost bled to death. After that, I had a change of heart about fighting a man. My brothers handled their business when it came to dealing with him.

"And no marvel: for Satan himself is transformed into an angel of light." 2Corinthians11:14

Chapter 7

Old ills

My brother, who was a few years younger than me, was killed. Too short! I was out at a club and was dealing with a female at that time. My man was at home. That night, we were watching the news and, on the news, it said that my brother was killed, but they said his first name wrong. I didn't even realize that it was him who had been killed.

I was high out of my mind. I came to my family's house the next day. They were in the yard and they told me he had gotten killed. I ran around the corner to my cousin's house and fell and hit my face on a tree. Delirious, I cried out so hard and could not believe that he was gone. They took me to the hospital but they would not let me see him, I was hurt so badly myself.

I was vengeful and wanted blood! I was trying to find out who was responsible for his dying. I talked to my cousins and found out what happened. I drove past the gas station where it happened and didn't even know that was the place where he had been killed. Seeing the scene with the police and knowing that they be tripping in that town where he died, anything was liable to happen. He was killed in October and his son and his mother and older brother were in a car accident that killed my brother's son and he was only 6 months old. Then, two months later his father died. My brother's life was too short. We had to take his son off life support.

The night we buried my brother we were drunk and throwing up with my brother's wife. When I woke up, I found my uncle on top of me, raping me at 26 years old, my dad's baby brother. Woke up with him raping me.

I called out for my brothers to come and help me. My uncle was an army vet and escaped up in a tree while everyone was running around looking for him. People saw him coming back out the tree.

I have been in all types of street fights, with police being hit with billy clubs, jars broken, being hit in the face with liquor bottles. I lost myself after my brother passed. I was mentally unstable after all these events. I was just hurt and numb. The funeral was overflowing with people, thousands of people, who came out to see him.

I was well respected in the streets, even when people pulled guns on my family. I became so hardened that I had no fear and was an all-out fighter once again.

I approached my uncle, finally, and found him in the street. I told everyone he raped me, then I punched him in the face and spat on him.

I was high one day and was smoking a primo, and I ran down the street and across the yard of a church and tried to get in the church. I got inside and looked up and there was an image of Jesus and a white cross. I fell down then and started crying out to God, asking Him to take it all away from me, the addiction, and I prayed I would never get high again.

I worked so hard to stay clean but old ills would come back to me time to time, battling with the addiction. I would battle with selling it or using it and then I was back on it, and my mind would trip, and I'd flush it down the toilet. I was battling with my addiction even going to church.

Let not sin therefore reign in your mortal body, to make you obey its passions. Do not present your members to sin as instruments for unrighteousness, but present yourselves to God as those who have been brought from death to life, and your members to God as instruments for righteousness. For sin will have no dominion over you, since you are not under law but under grace. Romans 6:12-14

Chapter 8

Deliverance

We ask God to deliver us from all debtors, problems, issues and even from our own selves, yet it never turns out the way we ask. It is on us to get the picture.

I was back in the street, dealing with a man who had the same familiar characteristics as the others, just an enabler and not good for me at all. I had prayed that prayer in that church but was at my wit's end. Nothing seemed to be working. I wanted off the drugs and out of the street. I wanted to be a better person, but how?

One day I was driving and got pulled over by the police and they said I had a case of welfare fraud. I could not believe that I was being locked up. When my court date came up, I only had a public defender and the only deal they were giving out was a guilty verdict. I had no way to explain myself, because truthfully, I could not remember what I had done. The judge was asleep up until the time he sentenced me, and he sentenced me to 18-24 months in prison.

I had done my first 90 days in the county jail. First day I got to the prison, all I could hear were all these women taking about new meat. Doing the cavity search, being searched with the gloves, and the things that they give you when you first get to prison, really set it in my mind that I was going to be here for 2 years of my life. The whole processing, from the moment I got into the prison, is something I will never forget in my life, from taking a 6-minute shower, to staying in quarantine 30 days until I was placed into the general population.

When I was walked into the cell after going through intake and into the main area, it was all eyes on me, new meat, and those women were not shy about what they wanted. I met my celly and she was weird, she just stared at me for the first couple of minutes. When she did talk, she asked me why I was in there and how long I had. I gave her as little information as possible, which prompted her to tell her story.

She said she had been arrested for killing 5 to 10 state police officers. She believed the officers had offended her parents, so she was out for get-back when it all happened. She was diagnosed with schizophrenia. She would crawl on the floor every night. She was on drugs. I had reported her and another prisoner and that was almost a death sentence. It was all about the code. Being new to prison I had no idea about the code.

There were so many evils occurring at that prison, in fact, in many, many prisons, whether it was girls getting called out to have sex with the guards and other abuses of power. There were allegations that girls would come back to their cells, crying and injured, late at night. And there were allegations that some inmates were doing in prison, the same things they used to do on the street. Drugs were plentiful. The police would bring them in, but not without a cost. Some inmates were doing hair and ordering clothes, just like living on the street. Even some women guards would reportedly take advantage of the prisoners also. I was approached by a guard who tried to take advantage of me. He broke my jaw and I bit him. I suffered for a couple of months with the broken jaw and they were not giving me any pain medicine, even when they took the wires out of my jaw. It was the worst pain I have ever experienced in my life.

I stayed to myself, I did not trust anyone, especially the guards. I was surrounded by women who had done some horrible things. I vowed, after I was done with my time, I was not gonna find myself back in prison. The thought of someone killing me had me on pins and needles, so I was uneasy at all times, and that was something I could not get used to.

There was a prison ministry and they would come to the prison and try to speak to us. I kept myself in the Word to bring some balance into my life. Every day was a constant reminder that I did not want to be there, under the stress of just prison life, but also under the lawlessness of the prison guards. If the guards were extorting the women, as was so often the case in prisons, these women had no voice.

Even when my celly and others were constantly preyed upon by the guards, they didn't bother me anymore because I was willing to fight back and die if need be. Prisoners could open up and tell their stories, as they did in so many prisons, but it was always the guards' word against theirs.

Just before I was to be released from prison, the situation came to light about what was alleged to be happening in prisons, especially women's prisons. In many such places, hundreds of guards were fired and even indicted. Some prisons were shut down and the inmates were transferred. In some places, that made the news! Finally, in 2003, the Prison Rape Elimination Act was signed into law by President George W. Bush.

Coming home from prison

When I was released from prison, I was happy coming home, but also nervous. I was out, not on parole, and trying to get my life back together. My plan was to get out, get a job, and take care of my children. Gaining my GED and learning some skills and reading while I was in prison gave me some inspiration to change what I was doing, or at least try. Released back to my old neighborhood, though, trouble was not hard to find.

I had spent the majority of my life fighting and winning all of my fights, and before I left, I had gotten into a fight. I fought a friend over $40 dollars. She hit me in the back with a sledgehammer and I hit her with a pitchfork. The day after, I got in a fight with her family member and she got the best of me. It was one of first fights against a female that I lost. I was outdone, she kept hitting me, and I had no real response until the fight was broken up. It seemed like my heart wasn't in the fight, either. This one I lost and I had to think about my future. I decided winding up dead over pettiness and someone stealing from me wasn't even worth it.

My daughter was pregnant when she was 16 so I knew I had to get my life together really quick. I applied for a job at a nursing home, but being a felon, I could not legally work for the nursing agency. Once my background check came back, the guy gave me a chance anyway and I proved myself. I did a good job and handled 21 patients by myself. He gave me that hall permanently and I was working doubles, three days a week, I was about to get my car, apartment, and take good care of my daughter and grandson.

Then, I got into a relationship that was not good for me. I noticed the relationship put me in a state where I started going backward, and I was not in love with this man. I reverted back to partying and dipping and dapping into weed and using powder again. I was still fighting, and my sister came and got me. Then I moved to the Deep South.

Be sober, be vigilant: because your adversary the devil, as a roaring lion, walketh about, seeking whom he may devour. 1 Peter 5:8

Chapter 9

Transitioning into a new life

In 2006, a lady told me about a man back in 2004 who had been trying to kill me. A man had been watching me while I was in that town and I had seen this man from the night before, sitting in my laundry room. I went back and found that he had taken some of my underwear. The man had taken some evidence that was supposed to prove he killed me.

That was a different environment, a different pace, and different faces. I was able to start over fresh and be whoever I wanted to be. I started working two fulltime jobs and a part-time job, and I even started going back to church. After four months, I moved out of my cousin's house and moved into an apartment complex and met a man.

We were good friends, but then it turned into a bad relationship. He was not into me. I was a rebound, but we got married. He was kicked to the curb by his children's mother. We stayed together in the church, where he was a youth minister and I was in the women's ministry.

A couple years later, at our 5-year mark, he decided he didn't want to be saved anymore. He didn't have any goals and didn't want to build anything with me. I felt that was a lot of time wasted, and he wanted to get high.

I went back into selling it during that time. I left him and met another man in 2011 and we started selling drugs together. A lot of back and forth with my husband during that time also, then I left him for good, and we divorced in 2014.

Once we went our separate ways, I decided I didn't want to sell drugs anymore. The man I met in 2011 and I were really cool, as friends, partners, and selling drugs together but he was a ladies' man and could not settle just for me. His heart was elsewhere, so we didn't make a stronger relationship because his family would intervene. He would stay out all night and I would lock the door. He got his ex-girlfriend pregnant and later would have two children by her. I decided to just stay to myself for a while after that. My taste in men was that I came on to them and was the one pursuing the relationships. I liked my men with some gangsta in them, and I liked intelligent and smart men. I depended on thinking that he would step up to the plate as a man. I thought wrong.

*****

"To loose the bands of wickedness, to Undo the Heavy burdens and to let the oppressed go free, and that Ye break every Yoke." Isaiah 58:6

I have become a motivational speaker, now ministering and consulting with men and women who are dealing with an addiction, the church would let us use their building and space to help these people.

My inspiration for not going back to the street was and is the love of my grandchildren. I wanted to be a better person after taking care of my grandchildren for four years and looking at the struggles that my daughter had with raising them. I didn't want history to repeat itself.

I felt I needed help, so I took the first step to get help, both with my drug addiction and mental status. I went to counseling for my domestic abuse and I've been free of domestic violence for the last two years.

I'm still in counseling for the rapes and molestation, and I've been diagnosed with PTSD. I am taking E therapy and went through the programs to become an advocate to help out girls, boys, women and men.

I now understand the importance of forgiveness and reconciliation. I have been able to be forgiven by my children and I have gained some understanding.

"Ye do I walk thru the valley of the shadow of death, I will fear no evil: for thou art with me: thy rod and thy staff they comfort me." Psalm 23:4

Chapter 10

Kept me covered

A church I was attending in my Southern town had a beautiful guest speaker one time, and as she was speaking, these words hit me harder than a fist: "Going through a process can kick your royal behind; it's like open heart surgery without any anesthesia."

Wow, such profound words! In her book she stated, "Pain is real; nobody should tell you not to feel it but misplaced or mismanaged pain can be dangerous. When people hurt you, you feel they should be punished, yes? Only the Lord can redeem the unredeemable. Forgiveness is your gift to give away to the very ones who damaged or almost crippled you."

In church, when this beautiful lady was finished speaking, it was book signing time. She periodically looked up with a smile as the line moved quickly, and when it was my turn, I greeted her. She looked up and said: "You have a lot of women waiting on you to encourage and minister to them."

As the fountain flowed down my face, I said, "I know this is God, 'cause she don't know me." While walking to the car and looking at the title of her book, which sent out a strong message, the flow of tears stopped. I realized that my life had been "altered not over!" That was Debra D. Winans who spoke greatness over my life that day.

As I look back on my life, as you've just read about it, having faith would have to be the only thing that got me through. I'm not saying that faith was everything that got me through, or that faith got me through everything, either. Sometimes I would fall, revert back to my old ways, old ills, and conditions would take me back to a dark place. Still, I had faith that always brought me back, no matter how far I fell, once I put my trust in God to cover me in my worst of times.

I am a firm believer that it's not what you say but what you do, it's the work and your word to yourself and God. No matter how many times you fall, GET BACK UP!

I look back over my journey and, yes, you could say that life was not fair and I was almost doomed from the start. All those experiences, either good or bad, made me who I am today, a walking testimony. It gives me hope that I can reach the next person who has gone through what I have, and I can show them that life can get better, if you want it to be so.

The course of my life could have taken a wrong turn so many times, but I was spared. What would have taken plenty of people out, left me still here standing. I know that I have a real purpose in life and my colorful background just helps me paint the picture better.

Therapy works. Giving the time to look back over things in my life and see them for what they were, the good, the bad, and the ugly, has given me a different perspective.

I see the story of Jesus and how He struggled in His time to minister to people, save souls, and ultimately pay the heavy sacrifice by giving His life for us all.

I always questioned, "Why me Lord? Why did I have to go through so much pain and anguish during my lifetime?"

I see my life now that my mission is to share my life with the world and use it as a sacrifice to speak to others, to help others.

The torment I suffered and survived has turned to normalcy, from the sexual, physical and emotional abuse being a way of life, to the struggle to survive, and to all the ways I tried to dull the pain.

I was a fighter in every way possible. Subconsciously, I was just letting out the anger, hurt and rage at the innocence stolen from me earlier in my life. It felt good, inflicting the pain that others inflicted on me, the brutality in my tongue and vicious blows that I would deliver from my fist, quenched a deep burning desire. I was an ever-erupting volcano and was ready to blow at any moment. I was truly a product of my environment, so desensitized to violence that it became a part of me that got me through and tore me down.

We never seem to understand what hurts us until we have that moment of clarity that we want to escape from what is paining us; we see it as a dead end, and we know nobody wins.

There is nothing wrong in breaking the silence out of love to someone who wronged you but holding grudges without showing it is not being real with yourself. That's just putting on a front and allowing it to manifest on the inside until it starts to show on the outside. It really takes more energy to be fake than original, generally speaking, to not be fault-finding or pointing the finger.

Accepting and dealing with what has happened in my life was a huge step and an unselfish one. We get locked into thinking about just us, just me, what I went through, and we forget we have the power to change it all.

The goal of the predator, the victimizer is to take away your power, to leave you feeling like no one will ever help you, feeling they will always control you and feeling you deserve that pain and domination.

Breaking the chains of abuse, self-worthlessness, sadistic behavior, dependency, and drug abuse is a long road, but it can all change when you are ready for your first step down that road.

The power is within you but how do we tap into that special power that is in us all? I believe in reinforcement. You must tell yourself over and over again, either with a pep talk, or by dealing with the reality of what will happen if you go back down that road.

Is it really worth it to get back to that low place?

Belief, trusting God that He will pull you through, and staying a student of the Word kept me going. Where the mind goes, the body shall follow.

It took some time and it still is an everyday battle to stay on course and not let down anyone who cares for me, and especially myself. One of the hardest things you will ever endure, after all the hell you may have gone through or may yet go through, is to rise again. I did it. I fell a couple times but got back up.

Conviction is knowing the truth knocks out falsehood's brains. When we are in trouble, or doing bad things in life, we have an internal battle between good and evil. I remember doing things I knew were a necessity in my life but I knew they were bad things. Whether doing drugs or selling them, I was in constant prayer. There were times when I would flush my drugs down the toilet and would not want to be in that life anymore.

Even after hearing the Word and knowing it, there was always conflict. During a particular time when I was smoking some drugs, I had a psychotic episode and this encounter really shook me. I could see the Bible on the nightstand, the pages flipping. That was a life-changing occurrence that made me more serious about wanting to overcome my addiction and cravings.

I liken my experience to Hell, in every form and way of that word. Overcoming has been a long road and I affirm to myself daily, "Greater is HE that is in me than in the world." Gathering strength is key to helping you get through it all, facing the pain, pushing past it, and practicing forgiveness.

The other part of taking this new, long road is going to see someone, talking to a support group, writing yourself a letter, confronting all your issues, and seeing a doctor also help. Therapy is necessary; it will help you push through and become better. Never give up! Always have a yearning for a better life.

ABOUT THE AUTHOR

Lady Façade's honesty is rivalled only by her faith in this, her first book, "A Story of Survival." It is more than merely difficult to read her account of her life but read it you must, because her present life and mission surpass all the demons, victimizers and perpetrators, she has survived, as well as all the wrongs from which she has been delivered. "If not for the love of Jesus Christ, I wouldn't be here," she recently stated. Her ministry and continued studies, her work with survivors of domestic violence and sexual abuse, and her motivational messages to girls, boys, young women, young men, and grown women and men are continually inspired and refreshed by her walk with the Lord, her daily time in the Word, and her love for people. "Sometimes we have to walk away, let go of those we have tried to love, but we do that by knowing that God's got them; God's got this, but we are called to love." Lady Façade is already at work on her second book based upon the present pandemic. Every word she writes is grounded in her faith that God does provide, and that is the abiding message she must share.

www.ingramcontent.com/pod-product-compliance
Lightning Source LLC
Chambersburg PA
CBHW050413030726
47503CB00006B/2178